About This Book

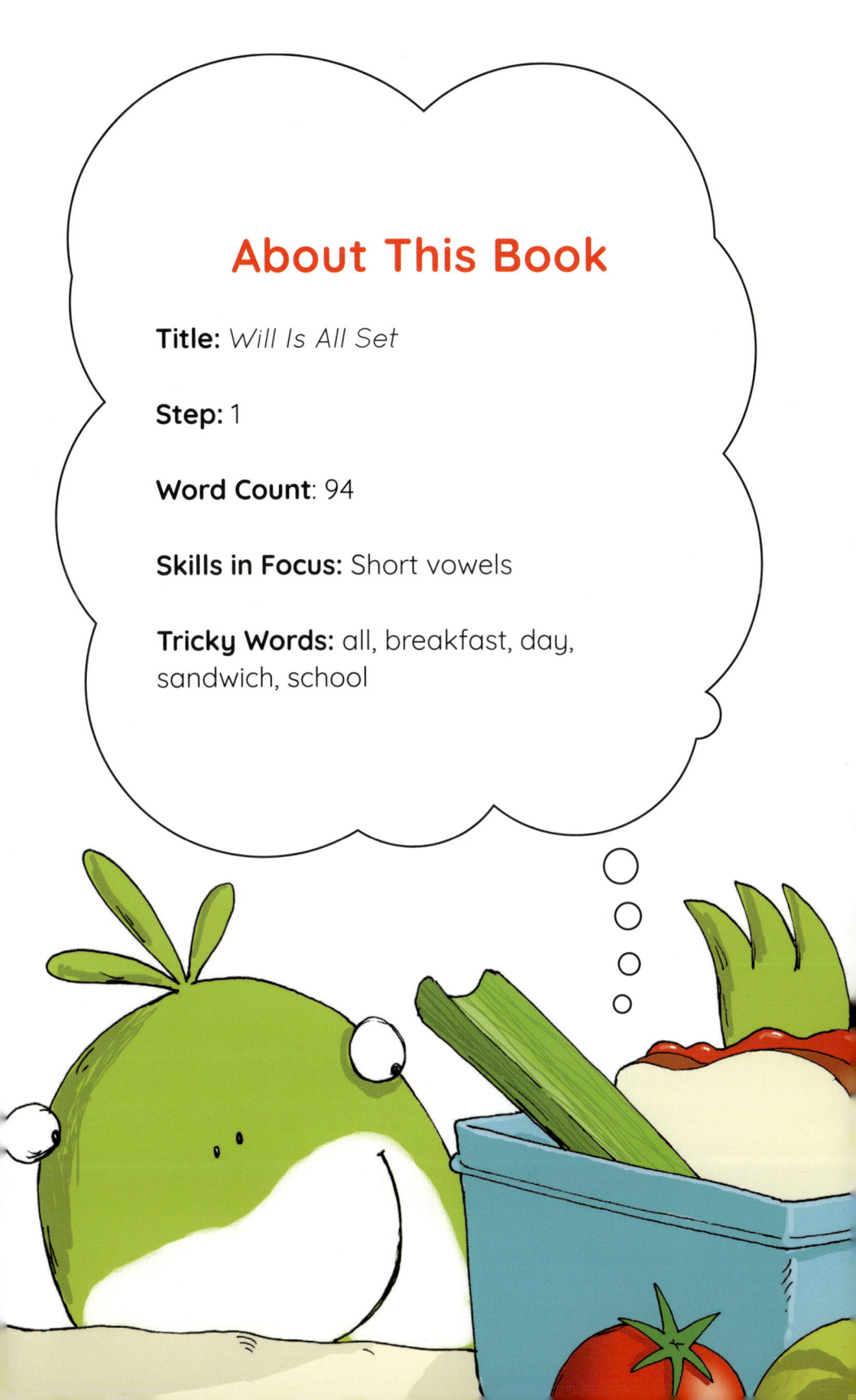

Title: *Will Is All Set*

Step: 1

Word Count: 94

Skills in Focus: Short vowels

Tricky Words: all, breakfast, day, sandwich, school

Ideas for Using this Book

Before Reading:
- **Comprehension:** Look at the title and cover image together. Ask the readers to make a prediction using background knowledge.
- **Accuracy:** Practice the tricky words listed on Page 1.
- **Phonemic Awareness:** Look at the title and help students blend the sounds. Call attention to the short vowel sound in the words *Will* and *set*. Practice taking apart and putting together the sounds in each word. How many sounds are in the word? What is the first sound? Middle sound? End sound? Browse the first few pages of text for additional short vowel sounds in the words *Mom*, *Dad*, and *sun*.

During Reading:
- Have the readers point under each word as they read it.
- **Decoding:** If stuck on a word, help readers say each sound and blend it together smoothly.
- **Comprehension:** Invite students to add to or change their predictions from before reading.

After Reading:
Discuss the book. Some ideas for questions:
- Discuss the sequence of events as Will gets ready. What does he do first? Next? After that? Last?
- Why do you think Will almost forgot to eat breakfast?
- How does Will feel about going to school? Explain how you know.

Will Is All Set

Text by
Leanna Koch

Educational Content by
Kristen Cowen

Illustrated by
Andrew Rowland

PICTURE WINDOW BOOKS
a capstone imprint

Dad, Mom, and Will.

4

WILL

Will is in bed.

7

"The sun is up," Mom tells Will.

9

"Let's get up and get set for school," Dad says.

11

Will gets his red pen.
Yes, it is Will's big day!

13

Will hops up.

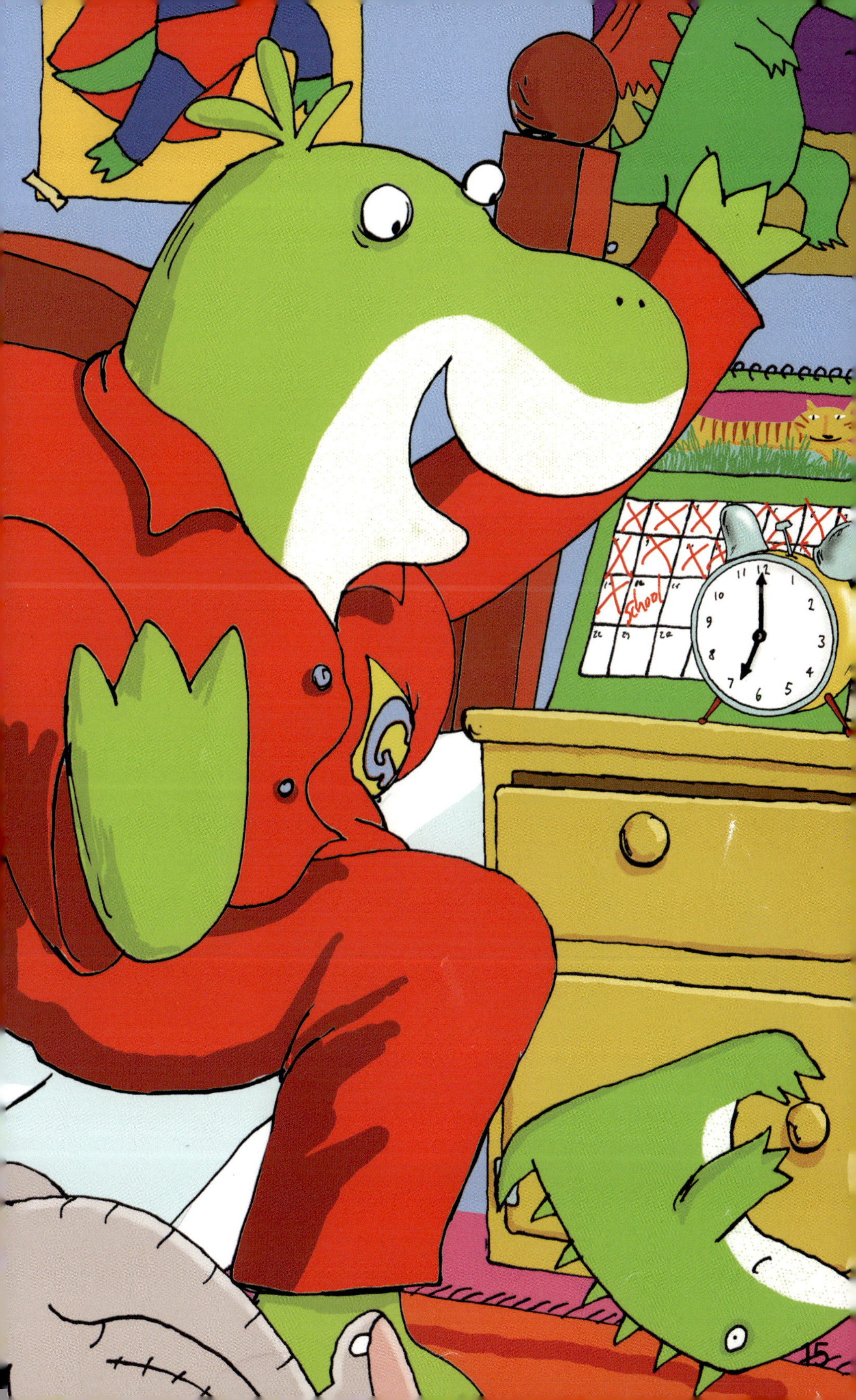
School

Mom helps Will get set.

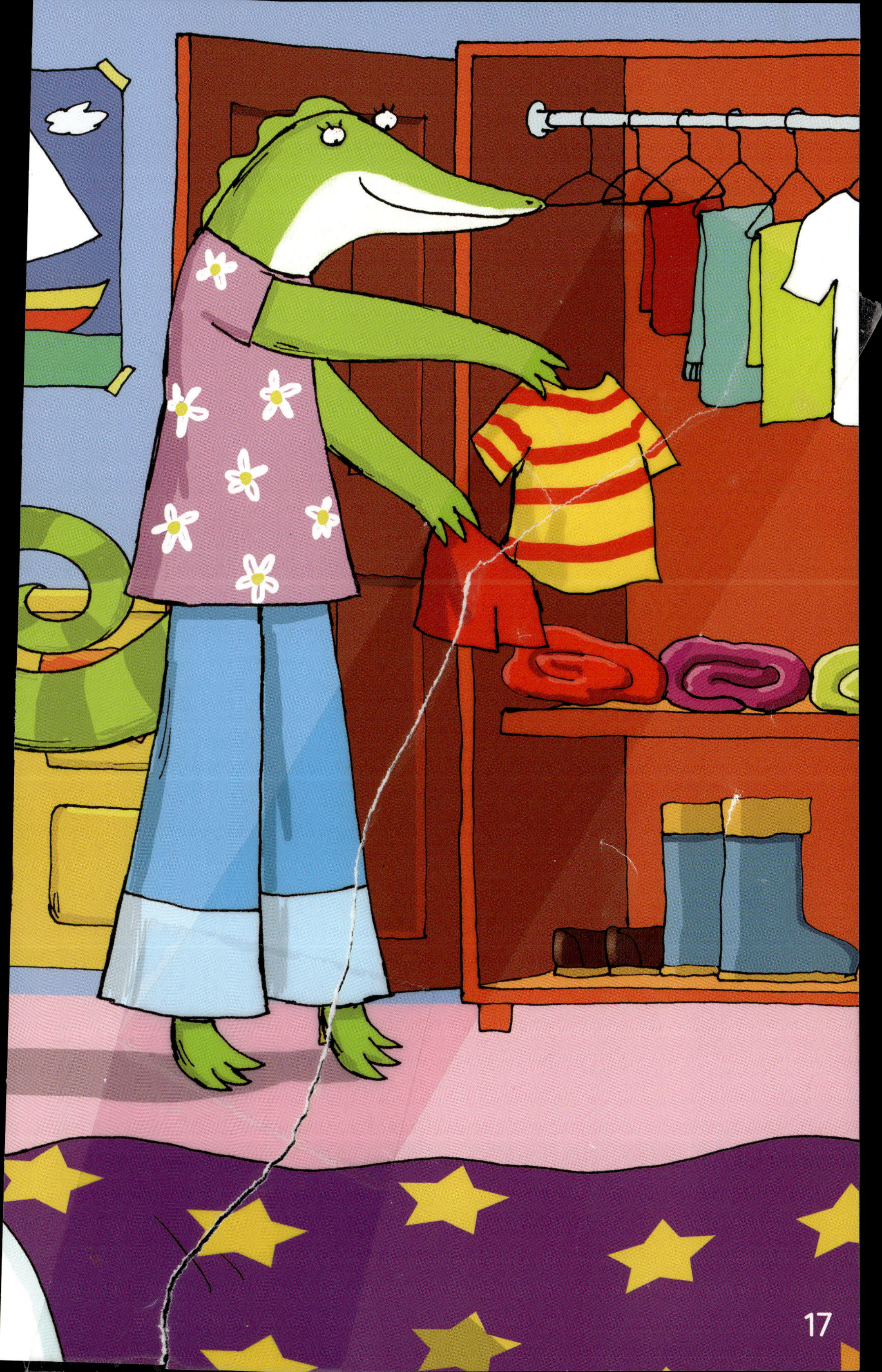

Dad puts pens in Will's bag.

19

Will packs a jam sandwich.

21

"I am all set," Will yells.
Will runs to get on the bus.

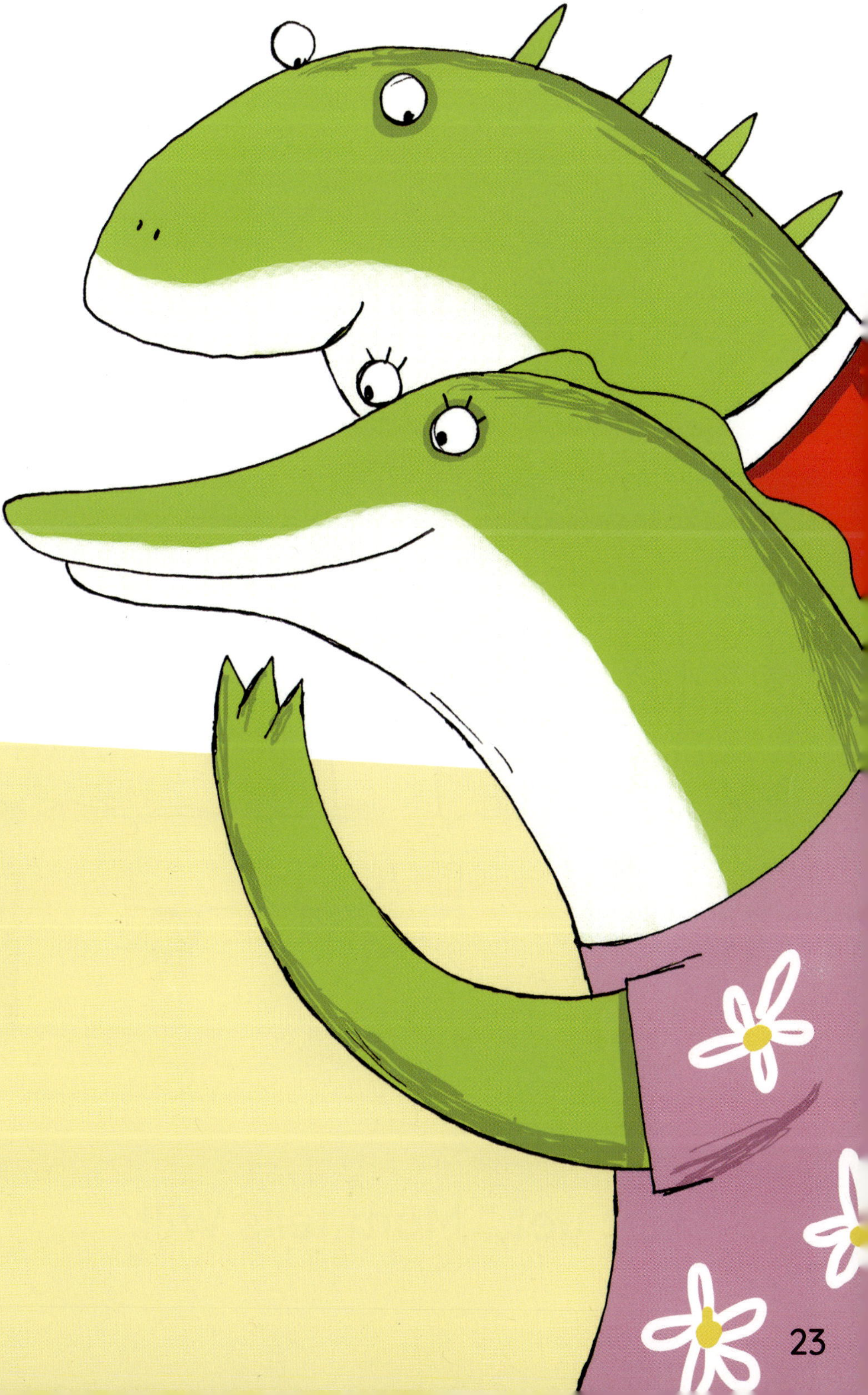

"Not yet," Mom tells Will.

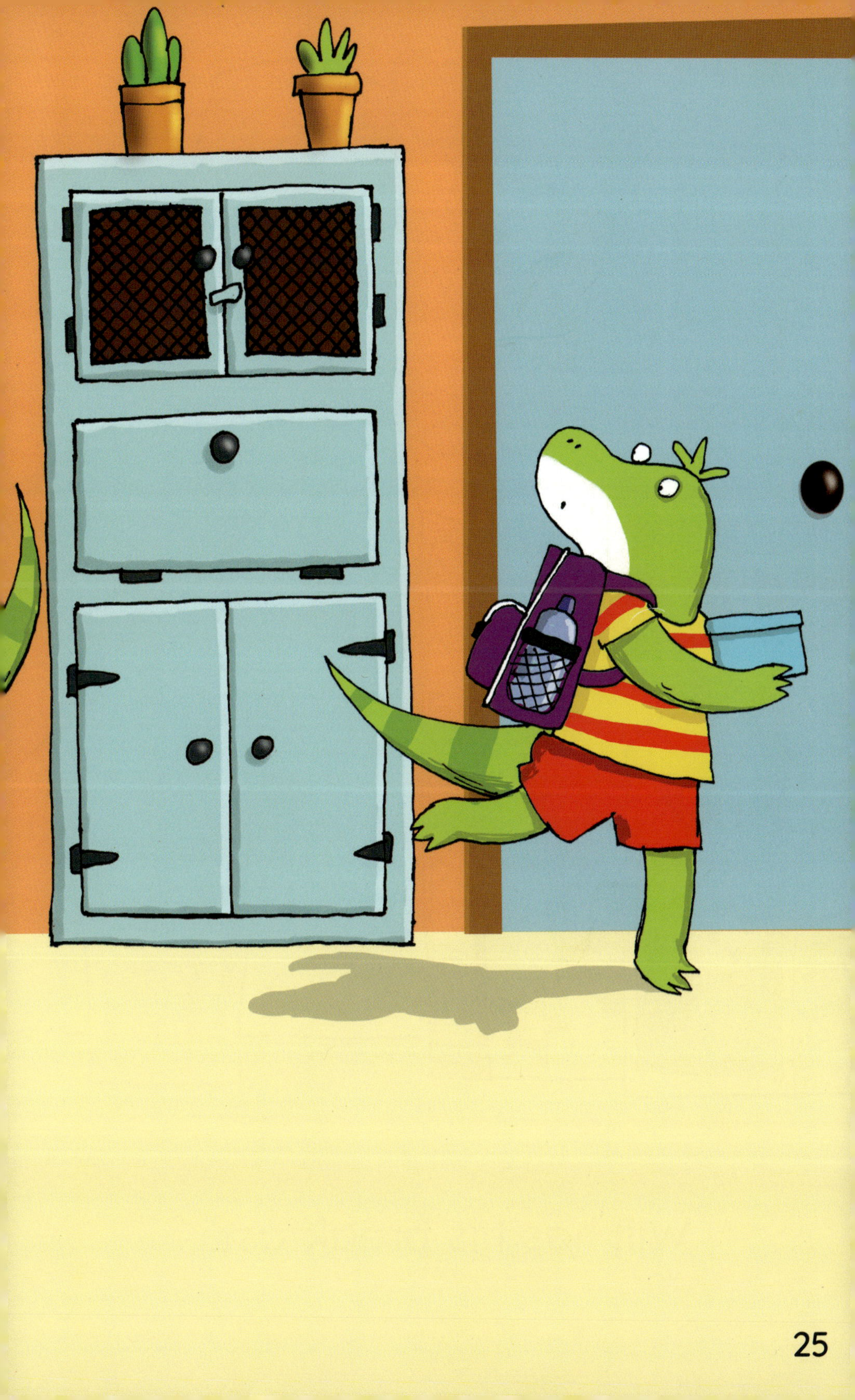

Will has his breakfast.

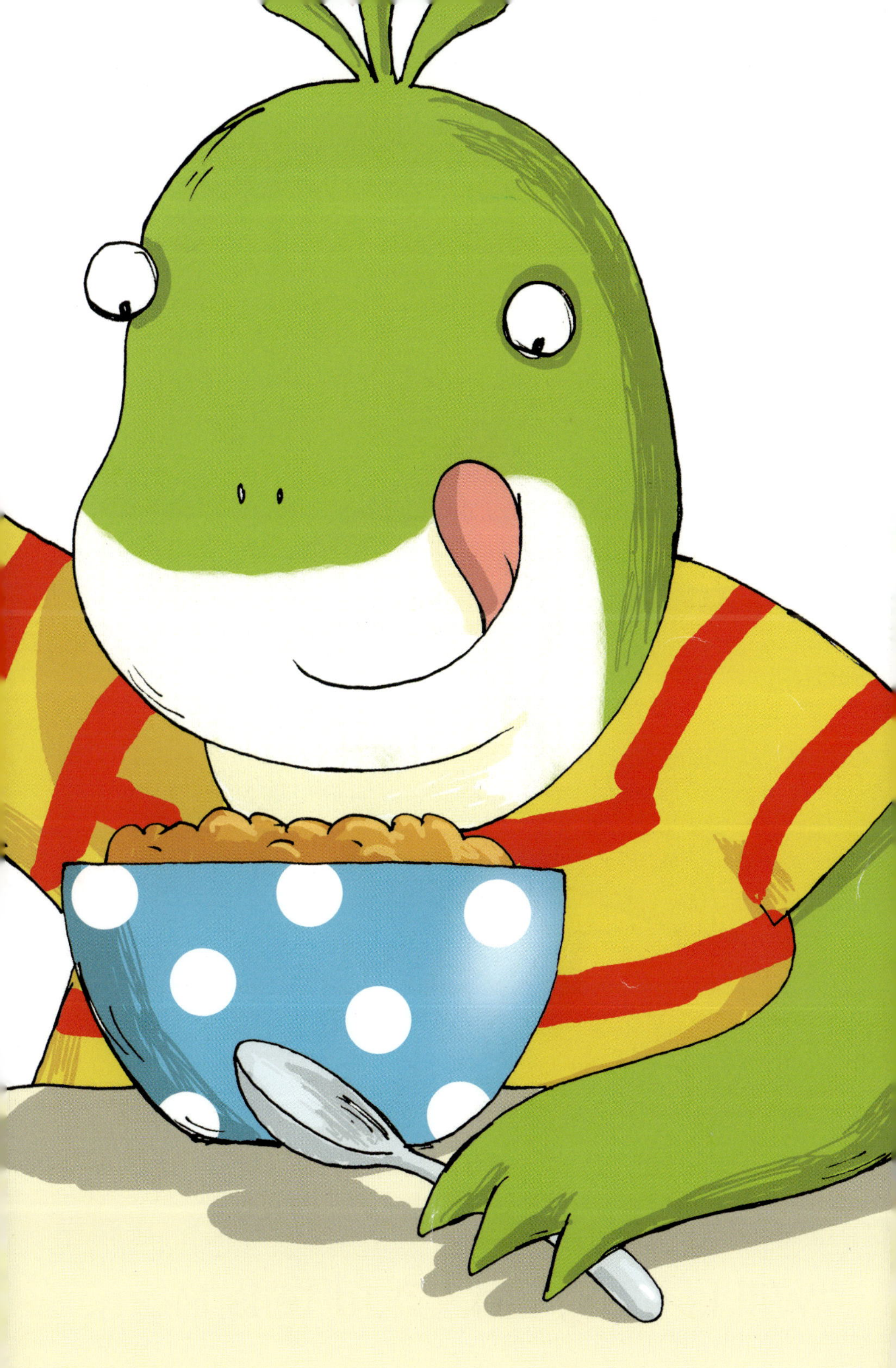

"Will is a big kid," Dad tells Mom.

Will gets on the bus. Will is all set!

More Ideas:

Phonemic Awareness Activity

Practicing Short Vowels:
Play "I'm thinking of..." with short vowel story words. Write the focus words on cards and place them for readers to see. Tell students you will segment the sounds of a word for the readers to blend. Say, "I'm thinking of a word with the sounds *m-o-m*. What word is it?" (*mom*) Once identified, show the readers the correct word card (or challenge the students to locate the word). Have students name the short vowel in each word.

Suggested words:
- b-e-d
- j-a-m
- n-o-t
- b-u-s
- h-i-s

Extended Learning Activity

Making Connections
Think about how you get ready for school each morning, just like Will. What do you do first? Then? Last? Separate your paper into the desired number of sections. Draw pictures of each step in your morning routine. Share with a friend. Discuss what you both do the same and differently.

Optional: Challenge the readers to label their pictures.

Published by Picture Window Books,
an imprint of Capstone
1710 Roe Crest Drive,
North Mankato, Minnesota 56003
capstonepub.com

Will Is All Set was originally published as
Little Lizard's First Day, copyright 2011 by Stone Arch Books.

Copyright © 2025 by Capstone.
All rights reserved. No part of this publication may be reproduced
in whole or in part, or stored in a retrieval system, or transmitted in
any form or by any means, electronic, mechanical, photocopying,
recording, or otherwise, without written permission of the publisher.

Library of Congress Cataloging-in-Publication Data is available
on the Library of Congress website.

ISBN: 9780756595920 (hardback)
ISBN: 9780756586140 (paperback)
ISBN: 9780756590284 (eBook PDF)

Printed and bound in the USA. 5757